Usborne Dinosaur Tales

The **Dinosaur** who asked "What for?"

Russell Punter

Illustrated by Andy Elkerton

Reading consultant: Alison Kelly

The Dinosaur Explorer Club is led by Sid and Maisie.

The club is Jen,

twins Bob and Ben

plus Stella,

Zack

and Daisy.

The Explorer Club is off to camp.

"Please help us load the van," says Sid.

But Daisy's feeling lazy.

"Hurry, Daisy," mutters Sid,
as he waits beside the door.

But Daisy drags her bag
along and loudly moans...

"We need to leave on
time," says Sid.

"Oh yeah? Who cares?"
says Daisy.

They reach the site.

Let's set up camp.

DINO VALLEY CAMPSITE

But Daisy's feeling lazy.

"Put your tents up," Maisie says. "We're in the field next door."

But Daisy rests upon her tent and loudly groans...

10

"What for?"

"We'll need somewhere to sleep," says Zack.

"Oh yeah? Who cares?" says Daisy.

"What next?" asks Ben.

But Daisy's feeling lazy.

13

"Help us gather wood," says Bob. He scans the forest floor.

But Daisy leans against a tree and loudly yawns...

"The fire will keep us warm," says Jen.

"Oh yeah? Who cares?" says Daisy.

"Let's fetch some water," Maisie says.

But Daisy's feeling lazy.

Maisie leads them to a well.
"Hold steady, while I pour."

Daisy flops down on a log
and loudly wails...

Stella says, "We'll need a drink."

"Oh yeah? Who cares?"
says Daisy.

Suddenly, it starts to rain.

"Take cover!"
hollers Maisie.

But Daisy's tent is still unmade. It's lying on the floor.

"I should have put it up at once.

And now I know...
what for!"

At last the rain stops
falling down.

Sid lights the
campsite fire.

They gather around to
warm themselves...

and watch the
flames go higher.

"Please let me dry off," Daisy wails.

I'm frozen to the core!

"I should have helped to gather wood.

And now I know...
what for!"

Daisy goes to find
a towel.

The water's boiled
by Maisie...

28

...to make hot chocolate
for them all.

"Just what I need,"
says Daisy.

But when she peers inside the pan...

There isn't any more!

"I should have brought some water too.

And now I know... what for!"

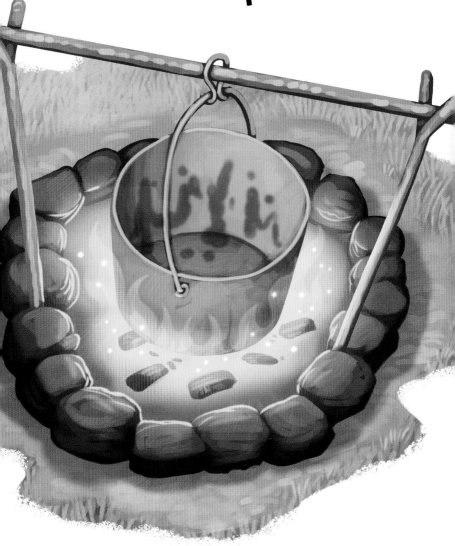

"We'll start the supper," Sid declares.

Daisy doesn't ask what for.
She's tired of being lazy.

She fills a bucket
from the well.

She fills up two, three,
four and more...

until she's out of puff.

"I think eight buckets ought to do."

She turns back to the site.

A spark has set light
to a tent.

Daisy shouts out,
"Follow me!"

The others cry, "What for?"

"Grab these buckets!"
Daisy cries.

They quickly take
a bucket each...

and race up to the tents.

Soon the fire has been put out.

"I'll finish supper!"
Sid declares...

and cooks a
steaming stew.

"Let me serve it,"
Daisy says.

"Please sit down,
be my guests."

"Hey, you saved the camp," says Sid. "You've earned a little rest."

"What, go back to my lazy ways? Just as I was before?"

Daisy simply gives a grin and loudly roars...

Series editor: Lesley Sims

First published in 2021 by Usborne Publishing Ltd., Usborne House,
83-85 Saffron Hill, London EC1N 8RT, England. usborne.com
Copyright © 2021 Usborne Publishing Ltd.

Look out for all the great stories in the Dinosaur Tales series!

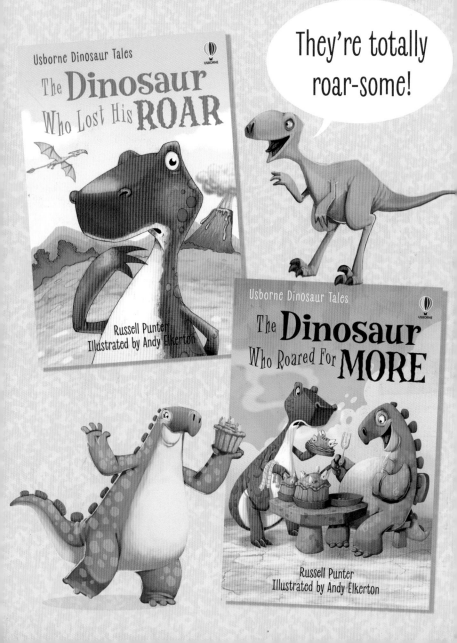

They're totally roar-some!

Usborne Dinosaur Tales

The **Dinosaur** Who Lost His **ROAR**

Russell Punter
Illustrated by Andy Elkerton

Usborne Dinosaur Tales

The **Dinosaur** Who Roared For **MORE**

Russell Punter
Illustrated by Andy Elkerton